ROCK YOUR WINGS

A story of friendship and flying.

Brandi Fill Books
4 Queensland Drive
Fredericksburg VA 22405
www.BrandiFillBooks.com
brandifillbooks@gmail.com

Ordering Information:
Quantity sales. Special discounts are available on quantity purchases by corporations, associations, and others. For details, contact the publisher at the address above.

Orders by U.S. trade bookstores and wholesalers. Please contact Tel: (360) 931-2558; Fax: (888) 599-2612 or visit www.brandifillbooks.com.

Printed in the United States of America

ISBN 978-1-365-12221-7

First Edition

For my children Audra and David
who were born to fly.
Also for the children of the Young Eagles Program
who dream of flight.

Maddie the Monkey loves to fly airplanes.

She likes to fly slow airplanes

and super fast airplanes.

She likes big airplanes

and small airplanes too.

Sometimes Maddie will see airplanes with stripes.

Now and then she will see them with stars.

Soaring high above the busy city

or low across the golden fields is so much fun.

Maddie can fly through small fluffy clouds.

She can also fly over very tall buildings.

*Lilly the Lamb, Mike the Mouse and Pepper
the Penguin are her very best friends.*

They love tagging along with Maddie.

Pepper and Lilly enjoy flying fast.

Mike the Mouse prefers to fly low and slow.

Every year Maddie flies her friends to their favorite air show.

As soon as the airport is in sight Maddie hears
"rock your wings"
and lands on the orange dot on the runway.

*Many other airplanes fly in behind
her and do the same.*

People from all around the world come to watch.

Maddie and her friends watch as the seaplanes splash across the water at the seaplane base.

They watch as some airplanes arrive in mass arrivals.

Pepper jumps up and down when helicopters swoop overhead.

Mike the Mouse watches as the airplanes take off and land safely.

*Lilly jumps with glee when the aerobatic
planes roll in the air.*

Maddie smiles when she hears the engines start up.

The propellers turn and they hum.

Mike and Pepper get a kick out of the deep rumble and the loud growl of the large engines.

*They all enjoy watching the
airplanes fly at night.*

*The runway lights are very bright and white
when the world is so dark.*

Airplanes fly around in loops with bright flashing lights and streaks of color across the night sky.

Beautiful music is played as the airplanes soar through sky.

Every year Maddie and her friends get to watch the air show with both new and old friends.

After the air show, Maddie flies her friends home.

As soon as they land they thank her for flying them to the air show.

Together, they help tuck the airplane into the hangar.

Before heading home Maddie looks up at the other airplanes in the sky.

She is very thankful to be able to share her love of flying with her friends.